# Big &SMALL™

# THE MISSING DINOSAUR

First published in Great Britain by HarperCollins Children's Books in 2010.

1 3 5 7 9 10 8 6 4 2

ISBN: 978-0-00-731984-8

A CIP catalogue record for this title is available from the British Library.

Based on the television series Big & Small and the original script, 'The Case of the Missing 'Saur' by Kathy Waugh. Adapted for this publication by Davey Moore.

© Kindle Entertainment Limited 2010.

Printed and bound in China.

HarperCollins *Children's Books*

# THE MISSING DINOSAUR

It was late at night and Big was sound asleep.
Small was wide awake. As Big slept, he snored gently.
And as he snored, his tummy went up and down.
And as his tummy went up and down, so did his
favourite toy dinosaur – T-Rex.

'Don't think I'm scared of you,' said Small, with his
blanket wrapped tightly over his head, 'just because
you have beady eyes and jaggedy teeth!' Just then,
Big rolled over and T-Rex came tumbling down the bed,
landing right on top of Small.

**AARRGGHH!!!**

Small ran straight out of the bedroom and slammed the door behind him.

Outside in the garden the next morning,
Twiba was in her tree, counting apples.

'Twiba!' shouted Small, from where he was lying, down on the ground. 'Be quiet! Can't you see that I'm totally tired and sound asleep!'

Big arrived, carrying his favourite T-Rex toy. He brought it up close to Small, which made him jump.

**'Argh!'** said Small.

'Hey, Small!' said Big, 'Do you mind watching T-Rex? I've got to go inside and I don't want him to get all lonely.'

'C-c-certainly!' said Small, nervously looking at T-Rex. 'H-h-happy to do it!'

'Thanks, Small!' said Big, heading off towards the house.

'It's not polite to make a Small have to babysit a ferocious monster,' huffed Small (just as soon as Big was out of the way).

Small couldn't bring himself to look at T-Rex's button eyes. Instead, he stretched out his leg and gave the soft toy a little push with his toe. T-Rex tipped backwards... and tumbled down a big hole!

Small looked down
at the stuffed dinosaur,
way down in the
bottom of the hole.
'Wooo,' said Small, his
voice echoing, 'you fell
down a hole!'

Small had an idea. He looked around. There was no sign of Big. He said, 'Holes are very dangerous. I think I'd better fill this one.' He began to kick dirt into the hole... and he kept on kicking until it was filled in – and there was no hole left at all.

Then he picked up a sink that just happened to be lying around and popped it on top of the mound of soil where the hole used to be.

'Ooops,' said Small. 'I dropped a sink.'

Small was about to walk away when a small voice from up above said, 'I saw that!'

Small looked up. It was Twiba!

'You didn't see anything, Twiba!' said Small. 'You didn't see anything, OK?'

Later that day, when it was night, Small was in his special spot at the end of Big's bed. He tucked himself in and said, 'Good night, Big!' Big did a big **YAAAWN** and said, 'Good night, Small!' And they both settled down to sleep...

Suddenly Big sat bolt upright. **'Hey!'**
he said. 'Where's my toy dinosaur?
Where's T-Rex?'
He switched on the bedside lamp.
'T-Rex!' he shouted out, 'where are you?'

'What am I going to do, Small?' said Big. 'I can't remember where I left T-Rex. What if I can't find him? What if I can't fall asleep without him? What if I can never fall asleep again? What if I just have to keep on talking like this, night after night after night after night...'

'After night,' sighed Small.

Small had an idea. He walked up the bed and sat down on Big's pillow. Big put his arm around his friend and snuggled up.

'Thanks, Small,' said Big. 'It's just until I find T-Rex, OK? Goodnight, Small.'

'Goodnight, Big,' sighed Small.

And Big began to snore... in Small's ear.

The next morning, Big was feeling gloomy. He sat at the piano and sighed a big sigh. He rested his chin on the piano keys making the piano go **KER-DANGGG!**

'I miss T-Rex,' said Big. 'Did you ever lose something that you really loved? It's terrible.'

Since he was sitting at the piano, Big sang a sad, sad, sad, sad song all about how much he missed his favourite toy.

Something about singing the song helped Big to remember something.

'I remember where I left T-Rex!' he said, jumping up and startling Small so that he fell over the back of his chair. 'I left him with you, Small, in the garden!'

Big ran outside into the garden and stopped underneath Twiba's tree.

'He can't have gone far,' said Big, looking left and right, 'I mean, he is just a toy.'

A small voice came down from the tree.

'Hey, Big! Are you looking for something?' It was Twiba!

'Shush!' said Small, catching up with his friend. 'Don't listen to her, Big! Twiba doesn't know anything.'

'Oh, yes, I do!' said Twiba, firmly. 'You pushed Big's toy into a hole!'

Small grabbed hold of Big's leg and held on tight. 'I think we should go to the beach!' said Small, very quickly. 'I really, really need to know how to swim. So come on, Big. Let's go!'

'Stop!' said Big. 'Twiba. What did you just say?'

Before Twiba could open her mouth to speak, Small butted in.

'OK! OK! I'll tell you!' said Small. He swallowed hard. 'OK, so there was this big hole. And, before I could stop him, T-Rex jumped into it!'

'You pushed him!' said Twiba.

'OK, so I pushed him – but then he fell! Into a giant hole! And, Big, as you know, holes are dangerous so I had to fill it with some dirt. And then I dropped a sink on it by accident.'

Big found where the hole had been. He dug at the ground until the hole came back. And, inside the hole, T-Rex came back too!

Big picked up T-Rex and shook off the dirt. Then he turned to Small and said in a sad, quiet voice, 'I'm very cross that you did this, Small. And I'm going to stay cross until you're sorry.'

Big walked back to the house.

Small folded his arms. 'Sorry? Why should I be sorry? Just because I took his favourite toy and buried it so he'd never find it. I mean, would YOU be sorry?' *

* Would you?

At bedtime, Small was in his special spot at the end of Big's bed. But he wasn't tucked up yet. He was sitting quite still and feeling sorry... for himself.

Big was getting ready for bed, and being extra especially careful to keep T-Rex close to him at all times.

'Hey, Big!' said Small. 'Which book are we going to read tonight?'

'I'm sorry, Small,' said Big, quite firmly, 'but I'm not talking to you right now.'

'OK, well...' said Small. 'Before you turn off the light, I just want to say...' He couldn't get the words out, so he whispered, 'I'm sorry.'

'What was that?' said Big.

'I said I'm sorry I buried your dinosaur! How many times do you want me to say it?' Small flopped back on the bed.

'Say you're sorry to T-Rex,' said Big, thrusting T-Rex at Small.

Small saw the dinosaur coming and hid under the covers.

'Small!' said Big, surprised. 'Are you **SCARED** of T-Rex? Is that why you pushed him into the hole?'

'Maybe,' shuddered Small, from underneath the blanket.

'Aw, Small!' said Big. 'I suppose he is kind of scary looking, so that's OK. But he's also quite cuddly.'

'Big. Could you please keep him in the cupboard at night?' asked Small.

'OK, Small,' said Big.

Small watched as his best friend walked across the bedroom towards the cupboard. And as Big walked across the bedroom he let out a little sniffle. And then a little sob.

Small felt terrible. He threw off his blanket.
'Oh, alright, he can sleep with us!' blurted out Small. 'Just make sure I can't see him.'
Big laughed, 'Hee hee hee! Thanks Small!'
He was very happy.

'Goodnight, Big,' said Small. 'Goodnight, Small,' said Big. 'Goodnight, T-Rex.' 'Goodnight, you horrible, horrible monster,' said Small, quietly.

Big switched off the light and they both fell sound asleep.

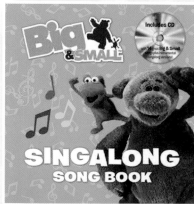